The Christmas Heart

and other stories of the season

Greg Borowski

Badger Books Inc.
Oregon, Wis.

ISBN+10 1-932542-25-6
ISBN+13 978-1-932542-25-7

This is a work of fiction. Any resemblance to actual persons, living or dead is purely coincidental.

Badger Books Inc./Waubesa Press
P.O. Box 192
Oregon, WI 53575
Toll-free phone: (800) 928-2372
Fax: (800) 928-2372
Email: books@badgerbooks.com
Web site: www.badgerbooks.com

For my mother,
who always let me put up the tree.

Contents

" 'You see,' Santa said, 'The moments are where the magic is.' "

"Back to a place where Christmas was always perfect and pure."

The Christmas Heart

and other stories of the season

The Night Visitor

As he sat on the living room floor, the only light coming from the fading fire and the soft glow of the Christmas tree, Mike Costello couldn't quite make out the hushed and hurried words that drifted down the hallway, but he could mouth them just the same. And for a brief moment, he did, picturing Laura at their son's bedside, balancing the open book on her knee, trying not to sound rushed, but nevertheless almost tripping through the words, ones she had read every night for the past month. "'Twas the night before Christmas, and all through the house ...." And Costello could picture

Nathan, too, his blond hair splayed across the pillow, the blanket pulled tight to his chin, wanting so desperately for the morning to come that he could hardly sleep now.

"*C'mon, Nate,*" he thought. "*C'mon, buddy. Just close your eyes.*"

The sleeping had been a problem of late, though Costello could hardly blame his 6-year-old son. Everything was still new to him — the city, the school, the neighborhood, the house. Indeed, the whole idea of winter was new, the way the snow came heavy and wet, the way the cold air turned his breath into cloud-like puffs on the bus stop. Throw the thought of Christmas morning into the mix, and of course it was hard to sleep.

Truth be told, all three of them had been unsettled by the move. They had been here since August, driving north after Costello's brother called to say their father was back in the hospital and the time to come was now. By the time they did come, a week later, once

Costello had set aside all of his cases and sufficiently tidied his life, it was too late, really. Too late to do anything but wait at the bedside, one week blurring into the next and the next and, soon enough, into the last.

By then, Nate could barely recognize his grandfather. He thought he was much too thin and weak to be the same guy in the photo on the mantel in the living room, the burly gray-haired man holding up a just-caught trout for the camera, his smile as wide as the faded blue sky behind him. Sometimes, he would stare at the picture, trying to see something familiar in the wrinkled face, trying to connect the past with the present.

They had moved into the old house as a convenience, but by the time the funeral came, Nate was halfway through first semester and Laura insisted they keep the house in the family for one last Christmas, never mind that a generous offer had come in and that his clients were beginning to demand more attention than he could provide from so far away and, didn't it just fit that this was the coldest December since he was a boy and the creaky old furnace never worked quite right and ...

As he thought about this, Costello realized his hands were squeezed into fists. He stretched his fingers open, shook his head sharply and blinked his vision clear. There was no sign of Laura, the low murmur of her voice still coming from the bedroom, a sliver of light from the open door slicing across the carpet. It was nobody's fault, really, that it was now 2:15 a.m. on Christmas morning and that no one was asleep and Nate's new bike, the one big indulgence of the season, sat in some 70 pieces scattered across the floor, demanding a mechanical touch Costello never possessed.

Costello bought the bike a week ago, slipping it through the back door on a Saturday morning while Nate was watching cartoons.

No one was more surprised than Laura when Costello put a finger to his lips, motioned her aside and opened the closet door just wide enough for her to see the box. For it was Laura who always did the Christmas shopping, often hunting for days to find just the right gift and then the perfect wrapping paper and ribbon to match. And it was Laura who always picked out the tree and strung the lights and Laura who organized the Christmas cards and baked tray after tray of cookies, carefully boxing them up for friends and neighbors.

And it was Laura who always knew just what Nate wanted. She would help him with his painstaking letters to Santa and then sit him down to write thank-you notes to all the far-away relatives that Nate could scarcely remember, including Grandpa Costello, who never failed to send a package.

"He's asleep."

The voice was one of relief. Laura stepped

into the room, the fire casting her shadow across the floor.

"Thank goodness," Costello said, not looking up.

He had made precious little progress since they got home from Midnight Mass and now stared even more intently at the jumble of parts. Just getting Nate to bed had been a production in itself. First, Costello had to explain that Santa must came later up north and no, Santa wouldn't forget where Nate was, and, yes, he would call the neighbors back home and have them tape a note to the door in case Santa needed help finding them. It wasn't until Costello picked up the phone and actually began dialing that Nate hugged his waist and ran off to bed.

"Yeah," Laura said. "He's out like a light."

Only he wasn't.

Nate had closed his eyes, yes. Closed them tight. He closed his eyes and pretended to sleep, gripping two plastic pedals from his bike-to-be underneath his pillow. He found the bike a few days earlier after he had come home from school and, as soon as Laura was busy at the stove, searched all of the old house's corners and shadows, basement to attic. He had to be sure Justin was wrong when he came over to the first graders on the playground and announced proudly that Santa Claus was, in fact, a fake, and if they didn't believe him, well, they should just go look under their parents' bed and figure it out for themselves.

Nate desperately wanted Justin to be wrong, so when he found the box holding the new bike — a red racer with a black seat and shiny handlebars — he slid his hand inside and pulled out the first thing he touched, the pedals. That, he figured, would be the test. For Santa would bring him a bike, because that is all he asked for and all he really wanted this year.

Yes, Santa would bring him a bike. And

that bike would have pedals attached.

With a little luck and a close reading of the instructions, the bike construction went smoothly, until, of course, the missing pedals, which happened to be the last step. Costello lifted the box and slid his arm inside. Nothing. He looked under the table. No. Under the couch. No. Laura picked up the box and set it down as Costello glared at her. "Already looked," he said, feeling around under the pillows on the couch. No. Laura grabbed at the pile of wrapping paper and ribbons where she was working. Nothing. She looked among the presents already under the tree. No. Near the firewood. No. She shrugged and offered a thin smile of support. Costello started to pound a fist into his palm, but she raised a hand. No. Nate was sleeping. Costello let out a slow, deep breath, then another, and went to the hall closet. Nothing. He went out to the car, returned and, with a frantic look on his face, reached again for the box. Still nothing.

"Did you ..." Laura said.

"Don't start," he said sharply.

"Can we ..."

"No," he said, louder now. "The stores are closed."

"Maybe we should ..." she began again.

"What?" he said quickly. "Call my brother?"

And, with that, the map of the conversation became clear. Costello turned away. Laura dropped her hands into her lap and lowered her head. No matter what, their arguments lately always found their way back to the same spot — his family and all the lost years, all the lost chances. Staying in the house meant wrestling away the memories, the nagging idea that things would have been different — would have been better — if they had come home sooner or if, years ago, he had not been so quick to leave. "No chance to mend it now," Costello had muttered a few days earlier. "Do you want to mend it?" she replied. "Did he?" asked Costello.

From the day she met him, whenever Costello talked of family — and it was rare — his voice carried a defeated tone. He'd talk about how his father always liked Jim, the oldest, the best, and how the two would go on their special weekend fishing trips to the cabin at the lake. "But you don't like to fish," she would say. And Costello would talk about how his father kept a scrapbook of clippings from Jim's days as a high school quarterback. "But you never played," she would say. And he would talk about how his father took out a second mortgage so Jim could go to college. "But you had all those scholarships," she would say.

She would say all of that, say it over and over, and she knew it wouldn't make a difference.

She knew this because of a story he had

told her only recently. It was about a day just before Christmas, when he was 6 and Jim was 8. He was sitting at the kitchen table writing a letter to Santa when Jim walked by, looked over his shoulder at the big wobbly letters and laughed. Jim said Santa didn't exist and he could prove it. Jim grabbed him by the arm and shoved him into the back closet, stepped in behind him and pulled out a flashlight. He clicked it on and pointed it toward the shelf high above them, the beam of light dancing across a red scooter, a baseball bat, a fat teddy bear, a bright yellow dump truck.

When Costello told the story, Laura knew he had decided that moment was the one that set the tone for all that followed, the one moment he carried with him even now. Laura knew this because the story came with this sober, very adult, reflection: "You know, it doesn't bother me that Jim took me into that closet," he said. "Because that's what kids do. But when I ran to Dad and asked him if there was a Santa Claus, he assured me there was. He said there was — and then he winked at my brother. And, you know what? Come Christmas morning, I had already seen all the presents that were under the tree."

"What I was going to say," Laura said, looking up, "is why don't we worry about this tomorrow."

She turned and went back to her wrapping and Costello stood in the doorway for the longest time, until finally she heard the creak of the stairs and his heavy footsteps toward the back of the house. It took another hour, although it didn't seem that long, and she set the last gifts under the tree, each reflected in the old-fashioned glass ornaments they had found tucked away in the attic. She positioned them carefully, blocking the bottom half of the bike, hoping to hold off — even for a moment — the inevitable task of explaining to Nate why Santa would leave him a defective present.

As she stood up, Laura noticed the photo of Grandpa Costello was out of place on the mantel. Nate was fascinated by the size of the fish his grandfather held in the picture and longed for a summer day to go out on the boat and catch one of his own. She adjusted the photo, thinking about how much Nate missed someone he never really knew. Then, just as she reached to unplug the lights on the tree, she heard a scuffling noise from the porch, followed by a soft tapping on a window pane.

She looked up with a start and saw a small boy peering into the living room, his face glowing softly in the bright string of lights. He was 5, maybe 6, and wore a red plaid hunter's cap, one ear flap missing. He smiled slowly, calmly. Laura raised her hand to wave, but before she could, the boy disappeared behind a fog of breath on the glass.

She rushed to the door, flipped on the

porch light and fumbled to free the lock, finally tugging the door open, the wind like ice on her bare feet. Nothing. No boy. Laura shook her head and stepped back inside. But as she closed the door, a tiny flash of light caused her to stop. It came from about where the boy was standing. If there ever was a boy.

Laura reached down and picked up two brand new pedals for a kid-sized bicycle. They were held together by a worn rubber band, a series of fat knots keeping it in one piece. As she turned the pedals over and over in her hands, their strips of yellow reflective plastic winked in the glow of the porch light.

And, though she would only remember it later, she did not feel cold at all.

The sun was barely shining through the icicles that hung outside the window when Nate ran into the bedroom, all breathless with excitement.

"Mom, Dad," he shouted. "Get-up-get-up-get-up, c'mon, get-up, Santa came, Santa came. C'mon, get up. Santa came and I got a bike and everything."

Costello rolled over, the problems of last night slowly coming into focus.

"Slow down, champ," he said, up on an elbow now. "We'll be down to explain in a minute."

"No, come now," Nate said, pulling at the covers. "Come see me ride the bike. I can ride it, I really can."

Costello swung out of bed, his feet hitting the floor with a thud. "What?"

"I can ride it," Nate said, his words finally slowing. "I can really ride it."

By the time his parents made it downstairs, Nate was on the bike, peddling it around and around the dining room table, ringing the bell with glee. Costello looked to Laura for an explanation, but all she said was: "Just enjoy it."

And that's what Costello did, a mix of relief and comfort settling over the day, the house warming a bit with every gift that was passed and opened. Nate climbed on his father's lap and asked where he rode his bike when he was a kid and when would it be warm enough to take it outside and, if he didn't fall down, could they please take the training wheels off? Costello kept glancing at Laura, wanting to ask where she found the pedals, but before he could, the doorbell rang and Jim and his family spilled into the hallway, the kids stomping the snow from their boots. There were more presents to open and, with the fire going strong and kids playing on the floor, the house felt familiar again. It felt like home.

It felt like Christmas.

Laura leaned in the doorway and took in the entire scene.

"Hey, Nate," she said finally. "Are there any little boys in the neighborhood about your age?"

"No," he said, barely looking up from the puzzle pieces spread across the carpet.

"None?"

"Nope."

"Is there a little boy who has one of those hunting caps?" she asked, trying again. "You know, the kind with the earflaps, only with one of the earflaps missing?"

"Earflaps?" Nate said, scrunching his nose. "Mom, no one would wear a cap like that."

"Yeah," Costello said, echoing Nate's sing-songy tone. "No one would wear a cap like that."

The two giggled like school boys and the others laughed, too. Laura turned back toward the kitchen, where a turkey was roasting and pies were cooling and Christmas dinner was starting to come together.

"Hey, wait a minute," Costello said. "Your grandfather had a cap like that when he was a boy. Haven't you ever seen the picture on the mantel?"

He reached for the photo and handed it to Nate. The picture in the frame now was black and white, a little blurry. It was a picture of a little boy, age 5 maybe 6, standing on a frozen lake and holding up a tiny fish he had pulled from below the ice. Laura looked over Nate's shoulder, certain the picture in the frame was a different one. But the picture was of a boy, a boy wearing a hunter's cap, one earflap missing, and a hopeful smile.

Laura couldn't be sure, but she thought it was the smile from the window.

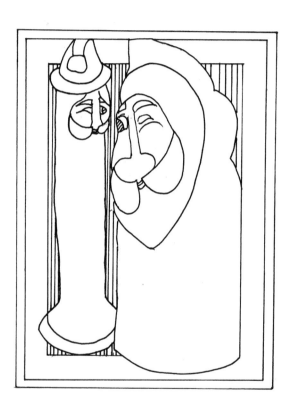

The Santa Suit

It was Christmas Eve, the windows already dark with the early evening, and Mitchell Brooks was busy undecking the halls. There were boxes everywhere. The tree was already stripped of lights, only the star left at the top of the droopy branches. In the background, the TV droned on, world news, the surest way to avoid any mention of the holiday.

It wasn't as if Brooks didn't like Christmas. He just didn't like this particular Christmas and the way it had played out, his wife still gone, their son with her, the big house feeling emptier than normal.

As he untangled a string of lights, there was a stomping of feet on the front porch, then the impatient ringing of the doorbell. Brooks went over and looked out the window. A delivery truck was parked at the curb, snow blowing in its headlights. He trudged to the door. As soon as he opened it, a package was thrust at him — "Here ya go." — then a clipboard — "Sign." — then the driver was back down the stairs, calling out "Have a good one." over his shoulder.

"Yeah," Brooks said, his voice flat. "Merry Christmas."

He tossed the box onto the couch, sending the cat scurrying across the floor, and returned to the stubborn lights. Brooks was determined to get the decorations in their boxes and the boxes in the attic before he went to bed, so this Christmas — the one that, technically, hadn't even arrived — could be over and he would wake up to just a plain old day.

That's what Christmas had become this year to Mitchell Brooks, the father of 4-year-old Jefferson Brooks, Jeff for short, but J.B. when it was just father and son, out as "the guys." The two were very close. They even had their own special signal — a double wink, first one eye and then the other — for whenever they were about to play a trick on Mom or lock in a secret between them. But Brooks had spent more time the past weeks talking to lawyers than his wife. Now it was Christmas Eve and Brooks had barely spoken to his son before Kate took the phone back and said they were late getting ready for the party, and why couldn't he just understand?

Now the phone rang.

Brooks brightened, expecting it to be J.B., and reached to pick it up.

"Hello."

The voice, though, was unfamiliar.

"Did you get it?"

"Get what?" Brooks asked, a bit startled.

"The box, of course."

"Yeah," Brooks said, suspicious now. He looked at the box on the couch. It was wrapped in plain brown paper and was tied shut with a piece of heavy string. There was no address on it, no postage. It was a wonder the box had been delivered at all. "Yeah, I got it."

"I knew they'd get it there."

"Who is this?" Brooks asked sharply.

"That's not important," the man said. "What's most important is who you are."

Brooks tried to place the man's age, but couldn't. The voice was old and young all at once. The man was quick and precise, but also somehow calm, as he ran through his request — a favor, he said, just a favor, a small one, tiny really.

"Listen, buddy," Brooks finally said. "I can't help you."

"Oh, but you can."

Brooks didn't respond. He just clicked off

the phone.

Curious now, Brooks picked up the box. The string pulled open easily, the paper fell away and, when he lifted the cover, the box revealed a heavy red overcoat with ornate brass buttons amid the fluffy white trim. Beneath the jacket was a matching set of pants and, of course, a stocking cap, with a fat white ball on the end. Brooks held up the coat and caught his reflection in the front window. Then he looked past the reflection, to the house across the street, where a door was opening and a family was being ushered inside amid hugs and laughter.

Brooks tossed the coat down on the couch and turned away. He shook his head, frustrated. So much for avoiding thoughts of Christmas.

The phone rang again.

"I hate to be a bother, Mitch." The man knew his name — and this time Brooks listened. "But I simply must ask you for that favor."

Fifteen minutes later, Mitchell Brooks was brushing the snow from his windshield and muttering to himself, wishing he hadn't done what he knew he would, which was to agree to the favor, no problem, glad to help, really. It was the same sense of obligation that kept him in the office late, sent him on all those business trips. Put simply, Brooks could never say no. It was his most endearing quality, ever helpful and concerned. But he had come to realize it was also his biggest downfall, the way it would pit work against family. "You're here, but it's like you're somewhere else," Kate would often say. "Can't you see how hard that is?"

As he finished clearing the windshield, a car rolled past and blasted its horn.

"Hey!" Brooks shouted.

There was the flash of brake lights and the car backed up. Brooks clenched his jaw. He didn't need this. Not a confrontation. The window rolled down with a hum and a small boy's face popped up. He wore a huge smile. "Merry Christmas, Santa," the boy said with a quick wave, as the car pulled away.

It took a moment to register. He was wearing the Santa suit.

Brooks waved back and tried to force a smile.

As he drove down the quiet streets, Brooks assessed the strange turn his evening had taken. He had agreed to put on the Santa suit, go to a nearby house and make a guest appearance. The man on the phone was never entirely clear about it, but apparently he had gotten sick or lost or delayed and couldn't do it himself. "And why should I do this?" Brooks had asked. "You'll see," the man said, then added: "Remember, whatever good you do, twice comes back to you."

That sealed it. The adage was as familiar to Brooks as an old blanket. It had been a favorite saying of his mother and he had taken to using it with his son. When he heard it, it was as if he had to help.

So on went the suit.

Indeed, the suit fit quite well. Brooks would need another 50 pounds to adequately play the role of Santa, but when he pulled on the coat, it was snug, as if it was somehow embracing him.

Brooks found the house, drove around to the back and clicked off the headlights so he wouldn't be spotted. As instructed, he slipped in the back door, holding the sleigh bells in his mittens to silence them, and at exactly 7 p.m., he burst into the kitchen and then the living room: "Ho, ho, ho."

Brooks, of course, was a hit. He posed for pictures with the kids — one girl and one boy — before admonishing them to get to bed early, to leave cookies out for when he came back on his rounds and, of course, to leave a few carrots for the reindeer, too. It was 15 minutes of pure family, only the family wasn't his.

As Brooks was walking out, the boy ran up to hug him.

"That was perfect," the father said, at the doorway. "Now you should get home to your family."

"I wish I could," Brooks said, quietly shaking his head.

When he got back in the car, a Christmas carol spilled from the radio, with its words of sleigh bells ringing and snow glistening. Instead of turning the music off, though, Brooks turned it up slightly. His heart felt a little bit lighter.

"OK," Brooks said, to himself. "Good deed done."

But his good deeds were not done.

At the end of the block, he saw a car stuck in the snow and helped push it out, leaving a look of astonishment on the face of the boy in the back seat. A bus rumbled past and

Brooks waved at the tired passengers, their faces brightening. Then he was spotted by a group of carolers and joined them for a few songs before begging off. And so it went, from one unplanned stop to the next and the next. At each, a little more happiness. He helped a man shovel his snow. Waved at the passing plow trucks, the police squads, the families headed to church. Later, when he stopped for gas, Brooks left with a gallon of milk to deliver to the old lady up the block, who the clerk said couldn't manage the snowy sidewalks.

Finally, after 20 minutes of coffee, cookies and small talk, Brooks excused himself. He was eager to get home. His back was sore. Legs, too. And he was starting to wonder how he was supposed to get the Santa suit back, whether the man would call again, or if he already missed the call or — worse — missed one from his son. As Brooks hurried to his car, there was a shout from the house next door.

"There you are."

Brooks turned. A man was on the porch, angrily waving him over.

"Over here." The man was frantic. "You're at the wrong house."

The driveway was filled with cars. A party was underway. Brooks could hear the commotion through the open door. He thought about it for a moment. The whole evening had been about doing good. Soon, he figured, some good had to come his way in return.

"I already called the agency," the man said, as Brooks walked up. "You were supposed to be here an hour ago."

Brooks adjusted his hat, buttoned the coat and stomped the snow from his boots.

"Sorry I'm late," he said, playing along.

When he stepped inside, the house was so warm it fogged his glasses. Brooks could smell the live tree, the burning candles, the gingerbread warming in the oven. There were lots of voices, all happy, and behind them joyous carols on a distant stereo. He could hear the crackle of a fire and, when he wiped his glasses clear, Brooks saw a giant tree, smothered with white lights, each blinking at its own pace, so the whole tree seemed to shimmer. He thought about his own tree, its branches already bare. And he felt lonely, lonelier than when the evening began.

"Hey kids, Santa's here," the man said loudly, guiding Brooks toward the tree.

As Brooks stepped forward, offering a less-than-enthusiastic "Ho, ho, ho," the path cleared and he saw a group of kids playing in front of the fireplace. He stopped.

There was J.B., looking up at him. His hair was as curly as ever, his eyes bright blue. He nervously bit his lower lip, never comfortable around strangers. He rolled a truck slowly across the carpet.

Brooks waved, but the boy didn't move. Other kids ran up to Brooks, hugging his legs and tugging him to the big chair by the fireplace, then begging for a story of reindeer or elves or life back at the North Pole. Afterward, each got a quick turn on his knee, but his son hung toward the back. Finally, someone nudged him forward: "Go ahead, Jefferson."

"It's all right, J.B.," Brooks said, reaching toward him.

The boy stopped, unsure of it all. Brooks froze, too.

"How do you know my name?" Jefferson asked after a moment.

Brooks just couldn't ruin it for him. As much as he wanted to hug his son, to pull the beard back and tell him it was all fine, it would always be fine, he decided to play out the role of Santa. He was so close, yet so far away from his son, from his past life, the one he desperately wanted back.

"Why, Santa knows everyone's name, of course," Brooks said, trying to sound jolly and loose, searching for just the right tone. Finding it, he pressed on: "Have you been a good boy?"

"Oh, yes," Jefferson said proudly. "My father always says, 'Whatever good you do ...'"

Brooks finished the phrase with him: "... twice comes back to you."

Jefferson looked up at Brooks closely. He studied his face, every detail and sifted through everything that was happening. Then he winked. First one eye, then the other.

And Brooks did the same.

"I knew it," the boy said, reaching up to hug Brooks, before finishing his thought: "I knew Santa Claus was real."

Brooks, pulled his son close, wishing he could let the secret out. As he did, he looked up and saw Kate standing nearby, a growing smile on her face, shaking her head at the unexpected reunion. For both, the easiness of the smile was the biggest surprise of the night.

Brooks took a deep breath and smiled back.

When he got home, Brooks flopped onto the couch, put his feet on a stack of boxes and, before he could click on the TV, fell asleep.

He woke the next morning to the insistent ringing of the phone, stumbled over to pick it up and began to rub his eyes. His head was pounding and he felt like he had a bad hangover, the worst in many years.

"Santa came! Santa came!" It was Jefferson, voice racing. "He knew my name and even knew our secret wink and everything. Now I know he's real."

"That's great, J.B., it really is."

"Did he come see you, too?"

"Well, he really only comes to houses with kids," Brooks said, then stopped.

He looked around. The house was again the picture of Christmas. The tree stood in the corner, covered with ornaments. The wooden Santa figures, some fat and some thin, were standing in a row on the window sill, an array of glass reindeer was back on the shelf. A layer of pine branches covered the mantle and three stockings hung below, as if nothing had ever changed.

The strange evening came back in a flash, and Brooks quickly looked down to check what he was wearing. No Santa suit. Just his flannel pajamas.

Jefferson was busy running through a list of all his gifts and Brooks thought he heard something about them coming home to visit, but that was lost as he continued his bewildering assessment of it all. There were no boots by the door, no box on the couch.

"What a weird dream," Brooks thought.

He sat down and noticed the cat was agitated, pawing at something under the couch. Brooks reached down and pulled it out. It was a long piece of heavy string, the string from the box, which — like everything else — was now gone.

"You know what?" Brooks said.

"What?" Jefferson replied.

"Santa did come," he said. "He most certainly did."

"I bet you got lots of presents."

Brooks thought for a moment.

"No," he said. "Only one. But it was the only one I really wanted."

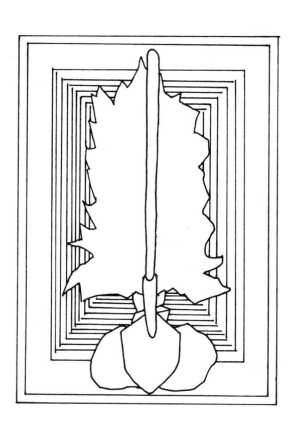

A Tree for Tomorrow

There once was a man who liked Christmas very much.

He had liked it since he was a boy, from the time he tugged the bow off his new sled, slid his fingers along the smooth steel runners and raced his brothers to the top of the hill, tumbling and falling in the fresh snow as they made the climb, then down to the bottom and back again, always staying outside until their woolen mittens were nearly frozen and the lights of the town blinked and gleamed in the valley below.

To him, Christmas was the clitter-clack of an electric train set, a stocking that bulged with promise, the sweet smell of fresh-baked cookies drifting up to his bedroom, nuzzling under the door and into the last moments of his dreams. It was hidden presents, letters to Santa and now, so many years later, it was the cards from a lifetime of friends that began to fill his mailbox with the first breath of December.

But this Christmas was different. The man had grown old and he was very sick. The doctors told his son they didn't think he would see another Christmas and sometimes they weren't sure if he knew this one was coming at all. But the man's son thought they were wrong, because every afternoon he stopped by the hospital and carefully read aloud the cards that had arrived in the mailbox that day and when he was done reading, his father always seemed a little brighter, a little more alert, a little bit happier than before.

"Remember," the son said one day. "Remember how you always insisted on buying a live Christmas tree? And how Mom always said those trees were too small, but you always had to get a live one because — what would you say? — because it was better to plant a tree than to cut one down."

The old man nodded and offered a smile.

Indeed, in all the time the two had spent apart, even in the long years after his mother died and December became more of a burden than a joy, his father always bought a live Christmas tree. And when the holiday was over, he pushed it in a wheelbarrow to a small piece of land he owned downtown and found just the right place to plant it, returning every week for months with a bucket of water to pour at its roots. Every year there was another tree and by now some of the trees were very tall. They almost made a small forest, the 50 or 60 of them, some spots shrouded in so much shade that come spring some patches of snow seemed as if they'd never melt.

The town was small enough that most everyone knew the old man, and they knew he was sick. They knew he was sick because a strange car was parked in his driveway, its license plates from out east. And the son, his face familiar if you stripped back the years, had not put the small tree in the front window. They knew the man was very sick when the ad appeared in the newspaper: "Prime downtown real estate. Wooded block. Close to City Hall and hospital." And they knew the man was getting worse when — earlier in the week — the construction fence went up around the land and the first bulldozer rumbled down Main Street, the smoke from its exhaust belching into the cold air.

They knew this because they knew the old man would never let his land be sold. They figured his son had looked at the land and saw its price tag, not its value. And, indeed, the son saw the price tag, but only because he also saw the medical bills that came mixed in with the Christmas cards each day.

So the son sold the land, but he did not tell his father.

Truth be told, he would have sold the land months ago, if he had remembered it even existed. The land, its deed found mixed in with the other records, was one of many childhood memories that had come back with his return to the house — the rocking chair by the fireplace, the faded snapshots on the stairway wall, the creak of the bedroom floor.

He remembered waking as a boy to the smell of coffee, but getting downstairs to find his father had already left for the foundry, breakfast dishes in the sink. He remembered running home from school with his report card, only to find his father asleep in the easy chair, the newspaper carefully folded at his feet. He remembered a room full of presents on Christmas morning and a father who never seemed to have time to play with him. And, lately, he had remembered the live Christmas trees and how, as a boy, he always begged and begged for a big tree, one that would sweep to the ceiling and sparkle with lights and candles, one to match the playground boasts of his friends.

And he remembered what his father always said in reply: "Their trees are for today. This tree, this is a tree for tomorrow."

"I remember those little trees," he said now, falling back into the conversation. "Maybe I can buy one and bring it to your room."

He looked for a glimmer of interest, a stirring, a connection.

"We can put it over in the corner."

But the old man just shook his head.

The son stood at the window, hours later, listening to the pump and hiss and whir of the machinery as his father slept. The son was tall and thin and on his own face the lines were starting to show. There was a time, years ago, when each visit home would end with an argument, but now the arguments were mainly in the son's head, always leaving the feeling he had let his father down — again — just by thinking them. The son was always searching for a moment, just one, to make things right. The sky had gone gray and he swiped his finger at the frost on the glass, trying to spot the old house in the distance. He heard his father cough, a rattling, shaking cough. His shoulders tensed, but he did not turn.

"Take me to see them," the old man said.

He meant the trees, the lot, the waiting disaster. The son cursed himself for ever bringing them up.

"But ..." the son began.

A nurse arrived and he was glad for the interruption.

"Another cold day, yep it is," the nurse said,

walking in with a burst of energy. "Little bit of snow, too."

The old man looked up and the son looked at his father.

"See," he said, gesturing toward the nurse. "I told you it was too cold for a walk."

"Take me," he said, stronger now.

After drifting in and out of the day, he had drifted in again.

"Always talking 'bout them trees," the nurse said. "Why don'tcha take him? What'll a little bit of cold hurt now?"

Before he could respond, the nurse took a knit cap out of the closet and tucked a scarf around the old man's neck. She helped him into the wheelchair, straightened the blanket on his lap and said, "He's gonna love seeing them trees."

The son took the nurse by the elbow and steered her into the hallway.

"Don't you understand?" he said, voice frantic. "The trees are gone. They started plowing the land today."

"No," the nurse said, calmly. "Don't *you* understand? Those trees are out there."

The son was irritated now, but he was also defeated. So he guided the wheelchair to the elevator and out the front door, its tracks snaking through a dusting of snow. He pushed the wheelchair slowly, hoping a few trees were left, maybe along the edge closest to the street, a few he could point at before they would turn around with an apology and the explanation the snow was simply too deep to continue on. As they got closer, he could see the fence and he could see his father's shoulders stiffen and he could hear the rumble of trucks and he could hear his father breathe deep and he could feel the tires slow in the snow, sliding off course as his own arms grew weak.

"Stop," the old man said suddenly, and his son stopped the wheelchair. It was growing dark now, the sky heavy, the shadows long.

The son started to explain, but the old man raised his hand.

"Turn me around," he said, and the son slowly spun the wheelchair until it faced the direction they had come.

The street seemed longer now. There were cars in a few driveways and along the curb the streetlights flickered to a dull glow.

Just then the Christmas lights on one house clicked on, bulbs blinking red and yellow and green and blue. They traced the edge of the window, framing a tree blanketed with white lights. Then, across the street, the lights on a house lit up, a shimmering blue. That house had a tree in the window, too. So did the next house and the one after that, each display brighter than the last. A car pulled into a driveway and a man got out, and shouted, "Thanks for the tree."

The old man waved back, the lights of the street reflected in his glasses.

"They must have got the one from the

corner," he said, looking up. "A good 15 years old, I'd say."

The son was bewildered at first, but soon caught on.

One by one, like dominoes down the block, the houses turned bright with lights, always a tree in the window. Some trees were tall and sweeping, others young and imperfect. All awaiting the sidewalk inspection, each tree a lifetime in itself.

This time, the son did not say anything and his father sat in the sudden light, his smile easy and his face, it seemed, a bit younger than before.

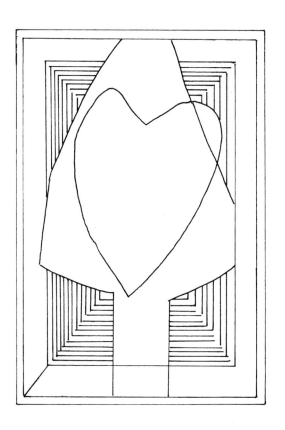

The Christmas Heart

It was two days before Christmas, the last day of school, and Billy and Andrew stood at the playground fence looking at the house across the street. The house was gray and the paint was peeling. In the front was a crooked fence and a wobbly mailbox and a giant old tree whose empty branches twisted up and up against the cloudy sky. The house was the only one on the block without Christmas lights in the windows. It did not have a Christmas tree or even a wreath on the front door. There was nothing happy about it at all.

"Does she really hate Christmas?" Andrew asked.

"Well," Billy said confidently, "my brother says she hates kids and if she hates kids, she must hate Christmas."

The day was cold and windy.

"Boy, I wish it would snow," said Andrew.

He looked up at the sky and tilted his neck so far back his cap fell off. Billy snatched it up and started to run away. The two ran across the playground, Andrew chasing Billy and trying to grab his cap back. Just then, the bell rang and recess was over. As they got near the door, the two saw Ms. Walters was already waiting, so they fell smoothly into line — boys on one side, girls on the other. Ms. Walters was the best first-grade teacher in the whole school. She had a nice smile and long brown hair and had promised that after recess they would all draw pictures to take home.

"Hello, boys," she said, as Andrew and Billy

walked past. They smiled up at her. "How nice of you, Billy, to pick up Andrew's cap," she said and winked at them.

"Oh, yeah," Billy said.

He gave Andrew his cap back and they ran giggling down the hallway to the classroom. Andrew went right to his desk and got out his crayons. He knew just what to draw. He drew a tall Christmas tree and on the branches he drew round ornaments, coloring them pink and blue and yellow and purple. And at the very, very top instead of a star, he drew a red heart. He wrote his name on the back and when Ms. Walters saw the drawing she held it up for the whole class. Everyone clapped and said it was just beautiful.

"You should give it to your mother as a present," Ms. Walters said.

But Andrew shook his head.

He knew what he wanted to give his mother and it wasn't a silly drawing. Every day on his way to school, Andrew walked past the jewelry store and in the window there was a Christmas tree covered with white lights and glass ornaments. The ornaments were shaped like birds and bells and stars and angels. And down at the bottom, at just the right height for a 6-year-old to see, there was a glass heart. It wasn't a solid heart. It was almost as if the heart was made of strings of glass that twirled around and around and came back together and twirled around again. Yes. That was the perfect present for his mom.

But the ornament cost $4.99 and even though Andrew had saved his allowance, he didn't have enough money.

Andrew looked up at Ms. Walters.

"No, my mother doesn't want another picture from me," he said. "She already has five pictures from me on the refrigerator."

"Are you sure?" Ms. Walters asked.

But before Andrew could answer, there was a shout and all the kids ran to the window. It was snowing, the first good snow of the year. Giant soft flakes drifted down from the sky, danced through the air and covered the playground in a soft blanket of white. The kids could not wait to go home. Ms. Walters read a book, but the kids watched the clock. The class sang Christmas songs, but the kids watched the clock. Ms. Walters got out another book and then — finally! — the bell rang. Some kids ran up to hug her, wrapping their arms around her legs, but Andrew and Billy went straight to the coat room and put on their boots.

In a minute, Ms. Walters came in holding Andrew's picture.

"You don't want to forget this," she said and handed it to him. Andrew took the picture, but he didn't say thank you. He just frowned and put it in his backpack.

Billy looked up. He was not a very good artist and had not drawn a picture to give to his mother.

"Can I have it?" Billy asked, then dug into

his pockets. "You can have this ball."

Andrew thought for a moment. It was a good deal.

"OK," he said.

They made the trade and then ran outside. They tramped around the playground in giant circles, spelling their names with their footprints. They flopped to the ground and made snow angels. They threw snowballs at each other. They laughed and chased each other down the street until, suddenly, Billy tripped and fell, his backpack sliding across the sidewalk. Andrew ran up.

"Get up, get up, get up," he shouted. He was out of breath.

"What?" Billy asked.

Andrew just pointed, his finger shaking.

They were right in front of the house. And if you were a kid at Middleton Elementary School, you did not want to be in front of that house. An old lady lived there. She had messy hair and a pointy nose and a crooked back and, some said, a heart that was so cold it was made of ice. She wore a tattered old cape and heavy, heavy boots and used a tree branch for a cane and when she walked, it sounded like this: Clump, clump, tap. Clump, clump, tap.

The kids called her Old Mrs. Crank.

Billy's backpack had spilled open and his papers were all over the sidewalk, blowing away in the cold wind. They tried to scoop up his pencils and crayons, but as they did, they heard the side door open. It creaked and then banged shut. They froze. And then they heard footsteps: Clump, clump, tap. They looked at each other, eyes wide.

Clump, clump, tap. It was muffled, but getting closer.

"Mean old lady," Billy screamed at the house.

"Yeah," shouted Andrew. "Mean old lady."

They made snowballs and threw them as

hard as they could at the house and ran away, each in a different direction. They ran so fast they didn't have time to turn around and see an old lady bend down and pick up a piece of paper from the snow, look at it and then pick up a crayon. Andrew ran until he got around the corner and then he slowed down, his breath coming in frozen puffs. Finally, he started walking again and took the ball out of his pocket and bounced it a few times in the sidewalk snow.

Then someone called his name: "Hi Andrew."

It was Hailey, from his class. She was sitting on the steps, watching her dad shovel the snow.

"Can I play with your ball?" she asked.

Andrew said yes and they bounced it back and forth a few times, until Hailey's dad said shouldn't Andrew be getting home and Andrew said yes. But before he left, Hailey asked if he would trade the ball for two toy cars.

Andrew thought it was another good trade.

As he walked home, he heard another voice:

"Hey, Andrew, where did you get those neat cars?"

It was Joel, who was in the third grade.

Joel collected toy cars and, after looking them over, asked Andrew if he would trade them for a new book. Andrew said yes.

Now, as he walked down the street looking at his book, its cover promising great adventure, he ran into Megan, another first grader. Megan looked at the book and saw it was one she really wanted to read.

"Would you like to trade?" Andrew asked eagerly.

But Megan said she had nothing to trade, only money from her piggy bank. So she gave Andrew $3.

As he walked, Andrew took the dollar bills and reached into his pocket. He pulled out two crumpled one-dollar bills — his allowance

— and he counted them slowly. One, two, three, four ...

Andrew's eyes lighted up. Five. He had five dollars! He ran to the jewelry store and pressed his face against the glass. He spotted the ornament, but then the lights inside went dark and a man started to lock the door.

"Mister, mister," Andrew said.

The man turned and Andrew held out his hand and showed him the crumpled money. They went back inside and the man took the ornament from the tree, removed the tag, placed it in a small box and carefully tied a gold ribbon around it.

"That will be $5.24," the man said politely. "With tax."

Andrew's face went blank. His lip trembled and he just about cried. He emptied his pockets on the counter, but all he had was a crayon, one marble, one nickel and three pennies.

The man smiled gently.

"It's OK," he said, handing Andrew the box. "But be careful. It's very slippery out there and the ornament is very fragile."

When Andrew went outside, the snow was thicker and it was hard to walk. He was going to put the box in his pocket, but decided it would be better to carry it. But just as he started walking home, he heard a sound in the distance. It was muffled, but it scared him still: Clump, clump, tap.

Andrew walked faster. He did not look back.

Clump, clump, tap. Andrew's heart was pounding.

It pounded faster than his footsteps.

Andrew started to run but slipped on a patch of ice. His legs flew up in the air and so did the box and then Andrew hit the ground and he heard the box fall, too. It fell with a crash. He sat on the cold sidewalk, tears running down his red cheeks. He opened the box and tiny pieces of glass spilled into his mittens.

"Little boy," someone called out. The voice was scratchy. It sounded like sandpaper.

Andrew looked up and in the swirl of snow he saw an old lady. She was tall and her nose was long and her hands were bony. She leaned on a twisted cane and there were heavy boots on her feet. Andrew gulped.

It was Old Mrs. Crank.

"Little boy," the old lady said again, but Andrew scrambled to his feet and ran all the way home. When Andrew got inside, his mother shouted not to run in the house, so Andrew stopped to kick off his boots and rushed upstairs to his room. Then he heard footsteps on the porch: Clump, Clump, tap. Then the doorbell rang. Andrew slammed the door shut. He didn't come out until dinner and then went back upstairs, while everyone else decorated the tree.

On Christmas morning, Andrew was the last one downstairs to open the presents. His mom got perfume, a scarf, gloves and lots of frilly things. They were almost done when Andrew's dad asked him if he wanted to give his mother her present.

Andrew waited before answering, a very, very long wait.

"But I don't have a present for her," Andrew said quietly. His voice was very small.

"Yes, you do," his Dad said and he reached behind the tree and pulled out a rolled up sheet of paper tied with a red ribbon. Andrew's eyes brightened.

"You should be more careful, young man," his Dad said. "Mrs. Kranklinberg saw you drop it outside her house yesterday and she had to walk all the way over here in the snow. When we see her in church this morning be sure to say thank you."

"Who's Mrs. Kranklinberg," Andrew asked, tripping over the long name.

"You know who that is," his father said. "She's the nice lady who sits in the back at church. She always smiles and waves when we come in. She lives right across the street from your school."

Andrew handed the picture to his mother and as she unrolled it, she smiled and a tear came to her eye.

"Oh, Andrew, it is so beautiful," she said and held it up for all to see.

At the bottom, under the tree with the heart at the top, it read: "I love you Mom, Andrew." The letters were crooked and wobbly, as if a 6-year-old had written them. Or else a very old lady.

"You know," Andrew's father said. "Mrs. Kranklinberg said she wrote a Christmas message on the paper, but I don't know what she meant by that."

Andrew just smiled.

His mother gave him a big hug and whispered, "I love it best of all." She hung the picture on the refrigerator, right at the top. As Andrew's brother and sister started playing with their new toys, Andrew sat on the couch thinking.

"Don't you want to play, too?" asked his father.

"No," Andrew said after a moment.

Andrew ran up the stairs and down the hall. In his room, he got out his box of crayons and a sheet of paper and sat at his desk. He knew just what to draw: A tall Christmas tree with round ornaments on the branches and at the very, very top a red heart instead of a star. He drew fast because there wasn't much time.

He had to finish it before they left for church.

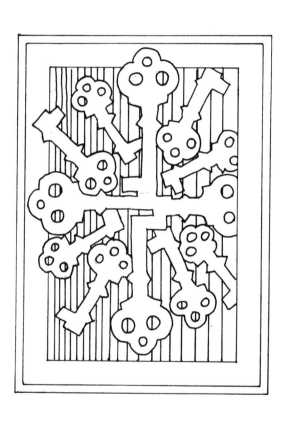

The Key to Christmas

They ran down the sidewalk, Jennifer and her niece, past the shop windows and snow-dusted cars, Maggie laughing and giggling as she tried to win their little race to the corner. They were off to the ice rink. Jennifer had come there so many times as a girl, she could still hear the slice of the blades and the bounce of the music, still see the giant Christmas tree in the center, its branches heavy with lights. And she could still taste the hot cider from the warming house, a dash of cinnamon on her tongue.

She slowed a bit to let Maggie win and waited for her amazed reaction. But when Maggie turned, she looked puzzled instead.

"Where are all the ice skaters?" she asked.

When Jennifer reached the corner, she saw Maggie was right. The ice rink was gone, replaced by a parking lot. No cars, just a heavy chain strung across the entrance.

"I don't know," Jennifer said, her heart sinking. "It must be closed."

"Not again," Maggie said quietly. "Not again."

Jennifer couldn't blame her. The ice rink was the latest disaster in a day that was supposed to be so, so perfect. The two were on their annual play date, a tradition for the day before Christmas, when Jennifer would fly into town, arriving so early she'd be waiting for Maggie to come down for breakfast. The two would always plan their adventure for weeks in advance over the phone, usually between elaborate stories from Maggie about how Santa Claus had come to visit her, stopping by her kindergarten class during nap time or at recess to let her pet the reindeer.

But this year, with Maggie in the second grade, there had been no such talk of Santa. Indeed, Maggie had assured her aunt there was no such thing as Santa. "Aunt Jen, I'm a big girl," she had said. "Big girls don't believe in Santa." And, truth be told, Jennifer didn't much want to come home this year. The visit, barely two full days, would hardly be worth the stress of squeezing it in. She had received a promotion at work and spent the days trying to keep up with clients, the nights trying to keep up with grad school, workouts, college friends, everything else in the rush of her life.

But when Jennifer heard Maggie say there was no Santa Claus, she could feel her niece's childhood slipping away. She decided she had to come home — and that this year their play date had to be absolutely perfect. They would do all of the things she did as a girl. They'd stop at Sweeney's to watch them make candy canes, visit the window displays at Foster's Department Store, then walk to the ice rink so Maggie could learn to skate.

Jennifer had even thought of the perfect gift — the treasure box she used to keep under her bed. The small box, made of polished wood with an old-fashioned lock on the front, held everything that was so important to a young girl: a four-leaf clover, a silver dollar that was real silver, sea shells from a vacation at the beach, a plastic ballerina from a birthday cake. Maggie would love it.

But the candy store was closed, Foster's had moved to the mall and now the ice rink was gone.

On top of all that, there had been the usual year-end crisis at work, and in her rush to pack for the red-eye flight home, Jennifer brought the box but forgot the key. She had lost the key so often when growing up her father finally tied it to an old shoelace and hung it around her neck, reminding her as he did: "You know, the little things mean so much. If you lose them, you lose everything." At least that's how Jennifer remembered it happening, it had been so long ago.

As they stood on the corner, the day falling to pieces, Jennifer's cell phone rang. It had been ringing all morning — a client, a manager, her sometimes boyfriend, more clients.

"It'll just be five minutes," Jennifer said, hand over the mouthpiece.

Maggie frowned.

"You said that last time," she said. "And it was really *five-hundred* minutes."

"Oh, it was not," Jennifer said, as gently as possible. She guided Maggie to a nearby bench and wiped a spot free of snow. Maggie crossed her arms and sat down. "How about if you try to catch a snowflake on your tongue,"

Jennifer said, then took the phone from her ear, stuck out her tongue and said, "Like this here." It came out: *"ike dith heah."* Maggie gave it a try.

And Jennifer, unsure how she could ever save the day, returned to her conversation.

Maggie sat on the bench and looked up at the gray sky, watching the snowflakes drift and dart to the ground, trying to spot the biggest ones, which, she figured, would be easiest to catch. She imagined she was inside a snow globe, one just shaken and alive with movement. The snowflakes fluttered down, landing on her eyelashes but not her tongue. Maggie tried and tried to catch a snowflake, but could never be sure she had one. What did a snowflake taste like anyway?

"I bet I could help with that."

The voice had come from nowhere.

It was warm as hot chocolate, comforting as a blanket in front of a fire. Before Maggie could look, the man snapped his fingers and — like that — the snowflakes stopped swirling in the air. It was as if the whole world had been put on pause. The traffic light was frozen. The cars on the street had stopped. A bus was stuck as it neared the corner, a puddle splashed half way into the air. Maggie looked at the man next to her. He wore a brown coat and a plaid scarf, but the white beard, red nose and twinkle in his eye gave him away.

She hadn't seen Santa in a long time.

"Hi," Maggie said simply.

"Why, hello, Maggie," he said. "I didn't think you needed a visit this year, but I guess I was wrong."

"I didn't," she said confidently. "I'm a big girl now."

"I know," he said, slowly shaking his head. "That's the problem."

"What do you mean?"

He explained how grown-ups can never

see Santa Claus, not because they don't want to, but because they are so busy moving from one thing to the next, this day to that, they can never stop and catch a moment. Only a child can take a moment, a moment like this one and see the whole world inside.

"You see," Santa said. "The moments are where the magic is."

They talked for a while longer, Maggie looking over every once and a while to see if her aunt had moved, but she hadn't. Not so much as a blink.

"For your Aunt Jen, this is no more than an instant," Santa said, trying to explain. "She won't remember it, but she will look back later and feel like she missed something along the way."

It was kind of sad, they agreed, this business of growing up. Soon enough, Santa said he had to get going — it was Christmas Eve after all, and he had work to do. But as he stood to leave, he turned.

"You know, I didn't get a letter from you this year," he said. "So, tell me, what do you want for Christmas?"

Maggie thought for a minute, scanning the world frozen in front of her. She saw her aunt, a frazzled look on her usually happy face. She looked at the bus driver, shoulders slumped, and at the passengers, faces long. All around her, snowflakes hung in the sky, like a million stars on a million strings. Maggie reached out and scooped one onto her mitten. It did not melt. She studied all of its angles and corners, sharp as glass yet delicate as lace. She tasted it. Sweet as sugar.

"I know," Maggie said finally. "I want Aunt Jen to get a moment back."

Santa smiled and thought to himself how wise children can be. How sometimes they could ask for nothing, yet their wish held everything at the same time. He nodded, then he winked at Maggie, snapped his fingers and — as suddenly as he had appeared — he was gone.

The bus rumbled past and the puddle splashed to the sidewalk. A car honked in the distance. And Jennifer, slipping the phone into her coat pocket, hurried back over to Maggie.

"I am so sorry, sweetie," she said. "Were you bored?"

"No, I was just talking ..." Maggie paused. "To this man I know."

"What?" Jennifer exclaimed. She turned and looked down the street, one direction then the other, all the horrible possibilities flashing through her mind — molester, kidnapper, drunk. "You know better than to talk to strangers."

"Oh, he's no stranger."

Jennifer was still doing her assessment. There was no one nearby, no one walking away. She looked at the bench. The spot next to Maggie was still covered with snow. No one had been there at all. Maggie kept talking.

"He said I should remember something to you."

"Oh, he did, did he?" Jennifer was playing along now. "And what was that?"

Maggie stopped and thought very carefully, trying to remember just how he said it, then in a very confident voice declared: "Little things mean so much. If you lose them, you lose everything."

Jennifer stopped cold.

She remembered the phrase, remembered it well. It was from deep, deep in her childhood. All these years, she had attributed it to her father, but it was from so far back, now she couldn't be sure who had actually said it. When Maggie said the words so exactly, it was as if a lost memory slipped back into place, only to quickly dissolve, fast as a snow flake, leaving more of a feeling than a memory, a feeling of comfort and warmth.

Jennifer looked at her niece, blonde curls

poking out from a stocking hat, and bent down to hug her. As she did, something caught her eye.

"What's that around your neck?"

Maggie shrugged and looked down. A silver key was hanging over her scarf, shining in the sudden sun. It dangled from an old shoelace, which was knotted several times. Jennifer took the key in her hand.

"Where did you get this?" she asked, almost gasping.

Jennifer wanted, for a moment, to believe it was magic, that there was a man, there was a miracle. But it had to be something else. Her sister had a matching treasure box. They both got them one Christmas. The same key would probably open both boxes. Maybe her sister, who knew about the left-behind key, gave it to Maggie, who didn't say anything but couldn't stop smiling. Yes. That had to be it.

In any case, it was a great relief. At least Maggie's gift would go just as planned on

Christmas morning.

"Well, what do you want to do now?" Jennifer asked.

Maggie declared she wanted to bake cookies for Santa, which meant a quick trip to the grocery store. As they walked to the car, Jennifer felt as if she had saved Christmas, at least for another year, while Maggie knew it was the other way around.

Jennifer smiled down at her niece.

"We'll have to hurry," she said. "We only have another hour before we have to get home."

"That's OK," Maggie said, looking up at her. "That's almost like forever."

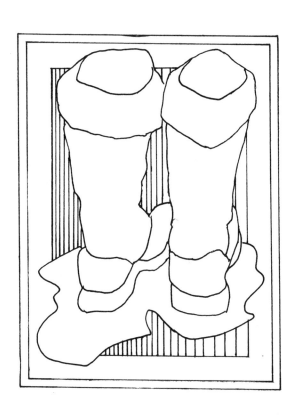

The Man With No Footprints

The highway was thick with snow. It growled beneath the tires and slapped hard against the windshield, the wipers twitching furiously but still lagging behind the whiteness. Inside the car, the defroster couldn't keep up, which forced him to make quick stabs at the fog every few miles.

"Some Christmas," he said.

He had searched for just the right tone of voice, the mix of irony and understatement that could somehow get the entire trip back on its proper footing, the tone that used to bring a smile. He could tell it hadn't worked even before checking her reaction. She stared out the window, shoulders squared, as she had for miles.

He wanted to say more, to say something different or maybe say the same thing in a different way, but he just gripped the steering wheel tighter. He looked in the mirror at his daughter, Sarah, who sat bundled in the back seat — too bundled, he thought, but was afraid to make that seemingly innocent observation again, seeing how it had turned into an argument hours ago. That was soon after they had left home, 5 a.m. sharp, driving into a gentle drift of snowflakes, a good omen for a trip that had somehow turned into another bad idea instead. The idea, back when it was new, was that they would, for the first time in years, make the three-hour trip to Grandma Malloy's, for the traditional

9 a.m. Mass. They would return to the town where they grew up, the church where they got married, to a past that seemed so much better than where they were now, free of tension and arguments, free of careers and compromises, back to a place where Christmas was always perfect and pure.

He had planned the trip for weeks, once she agreed it might make for a nice change, planned it down to the presents they needed to buy, the wrapping paper that was just right, the favorite cookies to bake, the clothes they would pack, the roads they would take and when they would arrive. But the light snow had become heavy, so heavy it obscured the mile markers, the exits, all the familiar landmarks. When he couldn't concentrate, he clicked off the music, but after a protest allowed the CD of Christmas carols to go into Sarah's headset, so the only sound now, other than the dull switch of the wipers, was the stray lyric when Sarah happened to know the words to a song. But they still were running late, which meant Grandma Malloy would soon be pacing in the back of church, the plans shattered, the day ruined. He saw her check her watch and tried to drive a little faster.

"There it is," she said, her voice even, impossible to read.

The words came too late and he pumped too hard on the brakes, the car slipping to one side and threatening to spin. He swung it even and the exit slipped past in a blur. He wanted to apologize, but knew she would ask why he was apologizing, so he just turned on the blinkers, slowed the car and eased off the highway at the next exit. The road was unplowed, of course, but after a few moments he spotted a restaurant parking lot where they could turn around. He pulled in, stopped the car, slipped it into park and turned off the engine.

"What are you ..." she began.

"She's melting back there," he said and climbed out, opening the back door and tugging off Sarah's jacket.

Sarah smiled up at him, lost in the music.

"We'll make it to church," he said, after climbing back inside, and she seemed to nod. The cell phone had been left on the counter back home, so they couldn't call ahead.

He reached for the key, turned it and got nothing. He tried again. Nothing but a moan. And again. The same.

He leaned his head forward, then back, staring for a long moment at the ceiling. Then he let out a slow deep breath. She pulled open the glove compartment and began flipping through the tattered owners manual. He saw her and tried again, cranking the key. Nothing. Not even a whimper of promise. He climbed out of the car and kicked at the snow in frustration. She stepped out, too, and walked around the car. She reached toward his arm, thought better of it and pulled her hand back.

In the car, Sarah looked out at the two and sang quietly to herself, "Better watch out, better not cry ..."

He raised the hood to a sharp hissing noise and turned his head away as steam blew loudly from a hose, spewing out a stink of green liquid. He lifted his hands in the air, unsure what to do now. From the start, she was always better in a crisis, able to ad lib when he lived by a script. So when she laid out a plan it felt good to slip into old roles. He would walk to the highway in hopes of flagging down some help, maybe a lonely state trooper or a truck driver on a trip home. She would try a pay phone at the edge of the parking lot and they would meet back at the car in 10 minutes, the amount of time they agreed, after some debate, a 6-year-old could survive without becoming too scared.

"Remember our first car?" she asked. The tone seemed warmer.

He offered a wry smile.

"I'm still trying to forget it," he said. "At least with a Beetle, we could have carried it to your mother's house."

She grinned.

"Heck," she said, "Sarah could have carried it."

He turned to say more, shrugged instead and trudged to the highway. Leave it there. Solid ground.

But there was no traffic on the highway and when he returned to the car, the snow had already smothered the hood and windshield. The wind had blown small drifts up near the base of the door, but he could still make out the vague footprints from where they had stood. There were his steps away from the car, the ones where she followed him, all the twists and turns of their argument. When he climbed into the car, she was already inside.

"Nothing's open today," she reported. "And the phone ate my last quarter."

He only muttered: "Figures."

"Why don't you start the car?" Sarah asked.

"No sweetie," he said, slipping into a soft smile and easy tone. "You see, the car isn't working."

She always liked the way he dealt with Sarah, sitting her down to explain the most complicated things. Once, after a late night at the hospital, she walked in to find him laying out an exceptionally rational argument, as if she were a student in one of his classes, about how she didn't need a new doll if she didn't play with the ones she already had.

"It'll work," said Sarah. "Chris said it would."

"Oh, Chris did, did she?" he said.

The name was a new one, the latest in

a series of imaginary friends, the sort the school counselor told them children create when they feel neglected during times of stress at home.

"*He,*" she replied.

"See, it's not working," he said, turning the key while looking back at Sarah. But the car coughed to life, the windshield wipers slicing through the snow as if nothing had been wrong at all.

"I told you," Sarah said and pulled her headphones back on, a picture of happiness, of pure and simple innocence.

They were already late, so he quickly turned the car around. The snow had begun to slow and now it almost sparkled in the early sun. When they neared the highway, he noticed a gas station on the side of the road, one he hadn't seen before — and a light was on. "I'll be darned," he said. They pulled into the parking lot and, although the faded sign read "Closed," he could see the shadow of someone inside. He got out, tapped quickly on the glass and tugged at the door. It swung open easily and the jangle of bells startled the white-haired man, who stepped from the washroom, wiping his freshly shaved face with a heavy towel.

"I'm sorry," the man said politely. "But we're closed."

"I know," he said, tripping over the words in his desperation. "But we really need some help. See I had a hose that burst and then the car wouldn't start and then it did and now we're late for church and ..."

The man simply nodded and pulled a heavy brown coat on over his dusty red shirt.

"I know what it's like to be almost home on Christmas morning," the man said. "In fact, I just stopped to pick up a couple of presents I hid here so my wife wouldn't find them."

The two stepped outside and, the engine

still running, the man lifted the hood. But when they looked, the hose that was burst just minutes ago appeared to be brand new.

"I'm not sure you even have a problem," the man said, slamming the hood closed. "In fact, everything looks just fine. Good day."

The man turned and went back inside and Sarah gestured madly from the back seat, waving at her father to get back in the car. He stood dumbfounded for a moment and looked at her anxious face, then back at the gas station door.

"One minute," he said, holding up a finger.

He followed the man inside, the bells jangling as the door bounced shut behind him.

"Hold on," he said. "What did you do to my car?"

The man turned from behind the counter. The patch on his coat read "Kris." He was old, at least 70, but his face was so calm and warm he appeared much younger. He seemed familiar, yet not quite familiar, like a word on the tip of the tongue.

"Your family is waiting," the man said gently. "And it's Christmas morning. You know, I always say that on Christmas morning, nothing else matters but family. It's so simple, but so right, don't you think?"

"Yes," he said, the words jarring him back to the present. "Yes, I suppose you're right."

He glanced out the window and could see that his wife and Sarah were both singing, the CD now playing over the loudspeakers.

"Yes," he repeated slowly. "Family."

The man reached under the counter for a candy bar.

"Here, give this to Sarah," the man said, leaving him bewildered by the simple gesture.

"Thank you, sir," he said, after a moment. "And Merry Christmas."

The man just smiled. He seemed to wink, then locked the door and clicked off the light.

It wasn't until after he handed the candy bar to Sarah that he realized the man had never asked his daughter's name. And it wasn't until they slipped into the pew at church — not a moment late — that he realized when he stepped out of the gas station there had been only one set of footprints on the ground in front of the car.

He reached for his wife's hand and was relieved when she squeezed back. He mussed Sarah's hair and repeated quietly to himself, "Merry Christmas, indeed."

Acknowledgments

This book is nearly a decade in the making. The stories inside are a product of a Christmas tradition of mine, in which I write a new short story every year and send it to friends and family with my Christmas cards.

Over the years, the Lansing State Journal, my former employer, and the Milwaukee Journal Sentinel, my current one, have shared the stories with readers in Michigan and Wisconsin, where they have developed a following.

Each year, they are photocopied and

passed on to others — by friends to their families, by family to their friends — to the point where, many months later, I will sometimes get notes from unknown people who got them and were touched by the message. They have become bedtime stories and stories shared over dinner, or read as a family on Christmas Eve, a night when everything carries its own special magic.

That sense of magic and wonderment, I hope, is what is captured in these stories. They are entirely fictional, but in the way that fiction feels like truth.

Thanks to Badger Books, especially Marv Balousek and Mary Lou Santovec, for helping bring the stories to a wider audience. And thanks to Jan Walczak, a longtime friend of the family, who contributed the beautiful illustrations, and her son, Tony Walczak, who eagerly assisted with the cover design.

My mother, MaryAnne, and my sister, Amy, are often the first people to read the stories. I am indebted to them, and to others, including my brothers David and Mark, brother-in-law Steve Ryan, and friends Tom Kertscher and Katy Flierl for suggestions and support.

Others who deserve thanks include Jim Higgins at the Journal Sentinel, a strong and subtle editor, and the artists there who have put their own special touch on the stories when they appeared in print. And the many co-workers, relatives and friends who over the years have said, "You know, these stories should really be in a book" — a list that if printed here surely would rival Santa's own.

I hope you enjoy them — and pass them on.

— *Greg Borowski*